ANDY AND THE SUNLINGS

DEVENS CHOICE

NISCHELAN NAIDOO

CONTENTS

Title Page

Copyright

Andy & The Sunlings: Devens choice.   1

Chapter 1: Checking in.   2

Chapter 2: A message   5

Chapter 3: Breaking the news   8

Chapter 4: Good to go.   11

Chapter 5: Time for an upgrade   15

Chapter 6: The big day   18

Chapter 7: The who's who   24

Chapter 8: Simmi and Dini   28

Chapter 9: Life blossoms.   32

Chapter 10: Time is up.   37

tHE END.   41

ANDY & THE SUNLINGS: DEVENS CHOICE.

CHAPTER 1: CHECKING IN.

Sitting here on a Sunday. Reminiscing about my adventure a little while ago now.

Given up my scientist life to accept a job that can pay the bills. No one will believe me that there is a race of advance people living inside the sun anyway. It would take special humans to do so. I wonder what that would be like. A planet with individuals that are accepting of other races, genders, and people with differences. I think it would be perfect. We are the most advanced race on the planet and that's constantly interacting in a global village.

Yet we cannot accept others or their differences to us. Utter nonsense.

Social media and the internet enable us to see the globe in any way we want. In doing so we must understand that we will be exposed to more.

If you are not aware of this. You do not deserve to

be apart of that global village. Wow, that got intense very quickly. MMMMM. I guess I have changed compared to my first adventures record. I've accepted I will never be a successful world-renowned scientist and that is perfectly fine with me. I am still a scientist at heart. That is fine for me. There are aspects to life and life itself that are more important. My sanity and health now take precedence overall.

I did share my adventures with those close to me once I had returned. Kavesh and my parents being super excited, Jevani and Kumesh very upset then gradually they too became excited and happy. They see that I have found my place in the world. I keep in contact with Nihal and the Sunlings very often. Nihal's gift makes it very easy. The communicator often beeps at odd hours as they never sleep so I had to limit my time in using it.

Its great to be back and living with a healthier routine. Surprising how a few days can change your entire life. It was a few moments shared with the Sunlings that changed my life. The world is huge but every single choice we make is integral to its survival.

So why am I logging this? Why describe my current situation? I've done what I wanted so why continue?

Well because the cause has changed, and I now find it very relaxing to ask myself questions in this manner. It allows me to record my emotions and reflect on them. It could be useful if ever I had to take my adventures to far of places at some point.

But for now, let it just be for my sanity. As per normal some tea and straight to bed.

CHAPTER 2: A MESSAGE

As I said my new routine finds me up early, tidying up my home or going on an early morning run. I have recently asked friends to join me on these.

Some, like Dru, are just remarkable with years of experience and insight far beyond my understanding. I'm grateful for this. Kavesh and Nishaan are close to my level of fitness and are excellent company. Always something interesting to talk about, usually never about the run but something unusual. This is something that I have come to look forward to recently.

After my morning run, I have my usual cup of tea and began to read my email. I replied to those that needed my attention and something caught my eye. The communicator Nihal had given me was flashing, unread message perhaps. Most likely.

I checked it to find this was the case. A message from Nihal. On reading it I saw that Nihal wanted me to contact him as he had something urgent to discuss.

What could it be that the most intelligent being I know needed to discuss with me?

I responded to find Nihal in excellent spirits after we spoke, he asked what had happen to The RG Show. I had to tell him that it was cancelled. I asked how he knew about this; he just laughed and said, the ball ,Andy the ball. Ahhh that crystal ball. No hiding from it.

Nihal then asks, "Ready for an adventure Andy?" suddenly.
I'm in shock. I didn't think I would return. Nihal might have need for me or just want company to share something new.

"Andy, aren't you going to ask me why?" Yes Nihal, why would I need to travel? What do you need?

I don't need anything, but I want you to travel to another star, I have a brother and he has no life in his solar system, I would like you to have a conversation with him and help him understand life and its purpose. He will get other visitors from other stars, but you will be the first of many.

So, what do you say Andy?

In shock and awe! Left with a dragging lip I mumble "yes off-course! "

Millions of years and billions of humans and again

I'm going to be the first of many, leaving my solar system to a new one. Hopefully to a hospitable, safe one.

So which sun am I going to Nihal? Not too far Andy, not too far, your first trip will be to me then I will help you to the next stop. Nihal tells me that he wants me to be ready in a few days to discuss why and how this all came about. And that I should pack as much as I did the first time, he will send all my nutritional requirements and environmental requirements to the other sun immediately so they may prepare for my arrival.

Nihal, such a complete being. Never forgets a thing. Wish I could have that level of insight and forward thinking.
Probably down to years and years of planning and nurturing a planet the size of earth.

CHAPTER 3:
BREAKING
THE NEWS

Not being one for traditional pleasantries I decided to invite my family and friends over. Making certain to tell each one that I need their assistance on a specific day as to not arouse any suspicion.

If I had said openly that I will be hosting a lunch or dinner, they would know immediately something was up.
So, the casual approach suits me better and would result in less drama. Which I am a huge fan of!

After speaking to Kumesh, Kavesh, my parents, Jevani they all accept the invite. Unaware of the others invitation. Now to break the news.

The day arrives and slowly but surely, they arrive at

my home. Jevani being first with my parents. They had fetched her along the way. Kavesh next as he probably assumed we would be watching football or discussing some new physics revelation. Finally, Kumesh, always fashionably late and utterly surprised everyone else was there as well. Immediately enquiring with Kavesh "Couldn't you have told me you were coming? " a very typical kumesh question.

Kavesh responded with "why would I think of you when I assumed it was for football, you know the premier league has just begun!"

Kumesh then knows somethings up. "Hey bestie, what's all this? Unlike you to be all secretive! Spill the beans."

Straight to it huh, mains it is, not even a starter.

Well anyway my folks and Jevani had tea and coffee, Kavesh was getting himself something to drink.

So I began, explain about my latest communication.

Go go go! Kavesh immediately says this is the greatest thing to ever happen to a human. He cannot contain his excitement.

My parents have a quiet gentle smile on their face. They probably know that I was going and just arranged all this to be polite.

Kumesh and Jevani were very apprehensive. Not

fond of science but very caring and concerned. Both of a very practical approach to life in general. They were processing and therefore they are excellent compliments to my lifestyle.

Both look at me almost instantly, Jevani saying go, I know you made up your mind, plus this I less risky, Nihal has catered for you.

Kumesh nodding in agreement.
Wow. That was easier that I thought it would be.
So on with lunch and football.

CHAPTER 4:
GOOD TO GO.

That evening, when my home was still, I sat quietly, and I began to imagine what this new sun would be like.Reflect on the composition of that solar system, that galaxy. Is there anything I need to be aware of? What about black holes? is the life span of the sun sustainable for life?

Ooooooh what a rabbit hole I decided to venture down.

Not good, not good. Immediately recognising that

these kinds of questions need to be discussed with Nihal, instead of making assumptions on my own.

I decided I needed a cup of tea. Chamomile, I think. After my tea a shower and straight to bed.

Waking to the sound of rain, in winter, very unusual for us to have rain this time of year. I guess I can't go for my usual jog today. Saturday mornings are the best as everyone else chooses to sleep in. Maybe I should have a haircut, considering my upcoming adventure.

A bit of grooming and self-care always leaves me feeling neat and tidy. A quick wash and cup of coffee and a I'm of to the barbers. Since receiving word from Nihal I have not removed the communicator. You never know what information could be passed on from the mother star or Nihal.

After my haircut I head home. The air feels so fresh. Probably because of the colder day. A shower, cup of tea and then the message. Nihal. Asking if I can be ready in two days. I guess a few days of leave wouldn't hurt. A truly personal day, I guess.

I inform Nihal that I would make the necessary arrangements, it was a Saturday so let me put weeks leave just to be safe.

Haircut, notebook, clothes, and my pillow. This is a

much easier adventure than my last. Especially since all has been arranged by Nihal in advance.

I guess all I need to do is wait for Nihal and for me to warm my machine up.

I nearly forgot about that. I had not really maintained it since returning from the Sun.

I remove the covers off it as I had stored it in my garage, looks like my weekend will go running repairs and maintenance.

After removing most of the dust all seems to be in order. I begin the initialization phase as I did the morning before I met Nihal.

While the machine starts up, let me have some tea.

With my cup in hand, waiting for the machine, I see a message from Nihal. I open it and see him asking why I am using that machine.

I reply, that how else I was supposed to travel. Nihal said not to worry about that. He gave me the communicator for a reason and that he will attend to all the travel arrangements. So, it looks like we are good to go!

CHAPTER 5: TIME FOR AN UPGRADE

Sunday comes around and everyone calls and visits. Knowing that I would be going soon. So, I tell them what had transpired the day before. I tell them all I know is that I'm going tomorrow and that I will not be using my machine.

Nihal then messages and this is a new type of message. It is almost like a download that we receive to update our phone software. It is very slow, and I see the communicator flashlights whilst doing so. I guess Nihal has something important for me.

A few hours later I go back to investigate and notice that the communicator has changed shape and has been really upgraded.

There is a new message from Nihal. Stating that he was sorry for the delay, but he needed to send me this upgrade to travel to Devens sun. I guess Deven will be my host on the new sun.

Nihal said that the sun is in fact Proxima Centauri. The closest sun to our own at 4.2 light years. The red dwarf classification means that this sun is cooler than others. It also has less intense light.

To us, this is excellent. Meaning we are going to assist Deven in increasing his suns output. To move from a red to a yellow intensity like our own sun.

Looking at the communicator I see that there is a new button. Labelled "Transport". I guess that's very logical and clear. The arrangements have been made. I've been upgraded.

Nihal must have set up this new device to allow me to travel to Deven sun by pressing this button. That's much simpler than me working out calculations to Proxima Centauri.

Nihal always thinks of everything. The rest of Sunday is relaxed. Spent eating and chatting to everyone.

The good evenings are said, and everyone returns home except Jevani. She and I watch tv and have dinner and sit in the garden sipping tea while the world around us quietens down and we go to bed.

CHAPTER 6:
THE BIG DAY

Up early as per normal. Who could sleep knowing that they could be on the biggest adventure in the history of man? Not me, that's for sure.

Out of bed and into the shower. Ready to go. Dressed and waiting in the kitchen having a cup of tea while Jevani begins her day. The excitement has added an extra boost this morning to my routine.

Jevani has tea with me, and we chat a little. I grab my things and say see you soon. She wishes me well and says to be safe on my journey.

I stand in the living room and hit the button.

No swoosh, boof or bang. Just a familiar silence and cool air.

"Welcome Andy, I've been expecting you."

"Hi Deven, I'm glad to be here." My immediate reaction to being greeted. In this case I mean every word of it.

In appearance Deven is very similar to Nihal. His voice is different, I can't quite put my finger on what is different, maybe it's because I find Nihal very reassuring. Deven also could be very uneasy as he has not had anyone other than his race visits him before.

Being the first here does add pressure as I will help him establish life in this solar system.

Wow. That's a huge task.

As with my visit to Nihal, the inner of this sun Proxima Centauri is a beautiful child like cartoon landscape. The homes and workspaces are almost identical to our sun's inner layout.

Deven tells me that because there is no life developing ,his Sunlings don't produce much output like Surya, Jas, Diya, Esmy or Franny.

Deven seems troubled he is very focused, and I can tell he wants to nurture life in his solar system.

Deven asks if I would like some tea. I never turn down a cup of tea. Especially if it will help in getting a conversation started.

"Nihal told me all about your love for tea". Said Deven.

"Yes, it's a nice way to share something simple and begin a conversation."

Most of those close to me have this habit as well. Whenever invited or visiting my grandparents or friends' parents we would often talk whilst sharing something to drink.

"So Deven let us share this age-old custom." He agrees with a nod and smile.

He tells me his yearning to have life on a planet in his solar system. Stating there are planets within the habitable zone. He says there composition is like Earth. Just that the output of his sun isn't as strong.

This makes sense. We need the radiant heat to nourish life. The one thing I did notice is that there are fewer Sunlings here compared to our sun.

On asking Deven why this is so, he explains he had sent them to the planets to investigate if life has developed.

This won't do. We need all those Sunlings here for a long time. This solar system is millions of years old. But billions of years younger than ours.

I guess Nihal is experienced hence him knowing this and working it out by trial and error.

So, I explain to Deven that he needs to get everyone back. He immediately moves to action. Calling for his second in charge Kae. Kae then sends a message to all the Sunlings from their communication hub. And slowly but surely Sunlings begin to appear.

Strangely enough you see Devens mood lighten. All the other Sunlings are so happy and playful. Running about and bringing life to the quiet and calm environment.

I look at my communicator and the suns output increased. It became warmer.

Deven asks how I knew. I told him. I have a family just like you. And you worry when they are away.

But with you your happiness directly affects the amount of sunshine this star gives off. So, for us to have higher sunshine all I needed to do was make you and the Sunlings happy.

That's why I asked for them to return.

"Thank you, Andy! I see why Nihal likes you and talks highly of you." Said Deven.

These planet nurturers praise me too highly. I'm just trying to be the best me.

Deven what are the questions you have about life and existence?

I know you have other beings coming here after me. Did you know what you want to find out?

"There are no others. Its only you Andy" Nihal said that, so you felt more comfortable in coming. Possibly because you are a scientist and want to help others discover new aspects of life.

Ok, so what do you want to know deven?

"Andy, what is most important to you?

What makes you happy?

What is your world like?"

These kinds of questions I have always asked myself

to relate to my situation and find out who I am in comparison to who I want to be.

"Deven, aren't you getting to far ahead of what you have to achieve? Considering that there isn't even a single plant or microbe on any of the planets in this solar system?"

"You are 100% correct and thank you for being frank with me. I ask you these questions because one day. A million years from now I will have humans on my planets, and I want my first encounter with humans to stick out very clearly in my mind."

This freaked me out. I will die and the person I am will be remembered by a being millions of years old.

Nihal must really like me to have sent me here to be the example for the next birth of life.

This was all too much for one day. Having spent the entire day in the main communications building we headed to Devens residence. Where I have some tea and had a rest. Time being non existent here just as with nihals sun.

CHAPTER 7: THE WHO'S WHO

Feeling rather drained the next morning as if I had not slept a wink. I slowly made my way to meet deven. Tea and what looked like porridge was prepared for me.

Then deven suddenly appeared and said, "I have been thinking a lot of what we had spoke of yesterday and I wanted to know how you become the person you are?"

My golden rule has always been "Just be a great human".

Doing the right thing even if you are the one who loses out.

Always remember a promise is a promise.

A few of the simple rules I live by Deven. These have helped me live the life I live.

Sitting here with you I could suggest a whole lot to look out for and what your world should look like. That would be unfair. I would limit the beings that live there their freewill.

How would you improve your world, Andy?

I would firstly form organisations to grow food at zero expense. No one should need to have to store food at home, the planet should be one huge orchard or plantation.

This will improve health and air quality.

I would add to improved air quality by doing away with petroleum-based fuel. Switching to hydrogen so that the planet is cleaner.

I would also insist that there is no purpose in hording gems and gold. They can be used in many industrial applications. Hording them for their beauty is frivolous. Serving no one any substantial good.

And the most important of all, make sure the water is of excellent quality.

Humans will evolve and find religion, lose it, evolve, find different ways to live and evolve further. Never really knowing that they are part of another race's happiness. Focusing on themselves and inadvertently destroying their home, chasing things that mean very little that is easily available in abundance throughout the universe. The inability to travel to those places limiting their resources and hence making it seem valuable to them. Looking after the planet that they have would sustain life and not just be selfish using what they want when they want.

Wow. Mind blowing. I see now why Nihal found me fascinating. I was the first out of billions on my planet, I could have found all the resources I ever needed in any galaxy I ever wished to visit. I could change the face of human history.

This is not me. Yes, I want to change the world. A piece of a planet will not help me achieve this.

CHAPTER 8:
SIMMI AND DINI

Enter Dini and Simmi two Sunlings here on Proxima centauri. They are much like Kae ,help deven with the main aspects of running the Sunlings daily activities.

They are different to all the others I seen both are very tall by Sunlings standards and slightly darker in skin tone than the others.

Deven introduces us and tells me these are his relatives and that they are almost the same age as he is.

I assume Deven is very close to them as they would have spent millennia together.

Simmi and Dini have a wonderful glow about them. They are special I can tell. They inform Deven that there was a discovery on the planet closest to them and I assumed that it was life developing.

Simmi and Dini leave Devens residence, he informs me that many Sunlings did not approve of Dini and Simmi at the beginning as they are different.

I asked how they are different, they are Sunlings. There wasn't any difference in them.

"Andy, you are remarkable, therefore Nihal sent you. You do not see colour or race or any other physical difference as a problem. Many others do not accept differences as easy as you."

Simmi and Dini are Sunlings with higher capabilities they are senior, as they have millennia of experience. They lived a long time on the mother star. Whereas many others did not. The younger Sunlings do not easily understand the existence Simmi and Dini have experienced. They are different but do not harm anyone but show the most love of all. They glow because of that love. They are the happiest here because they care for all the others and me.

Kae now enters, happy and joyful, literally bouncing as he walks.

"Deven, you did it, Deven you did it" he screams in joy.

No Kae, we did it. It was Andy's suggestion to bring every single Sunlings back and all of you radiating wonderfully to warm the planet enough so that life can develop.

Kae smiles and says "you are to kind Deven. I'm just so happy! The life we saw was basic, single celled organisms"

Oh, was it an amoeba?" I interject rudely.

Yes, exclaimed Kae.

"Those where the first forms of life on planet earth as well. They still occur to this day, millions of years later."

"Andy aren't you scared to hurt or kill a life form?" asked Kae.

"Yes, most definitely. I was taught that all life is precious. Their health is linked directly to my own. Trees produce oxygen and remove carbon di oxide, those trees shelter animals, whose animals help trees pollinate and spread seeds, the trees help produce rain and so on and so on. The planet is one big habitat"

David Attenborough, Jane Goodall, Steve Erwin, Bear Grylls and Greta Thunberg and millions of others have all made massive strides in raising awareness. Humans on my planet have potential for greatness. Realising that each is as wealthy as the next. He or she has only a very limited time on that planet. We do not live the vast eternities that you all do.

When your sole purpose is to help the next generation then an only then will man be successful.

CHAPTER 9: LIFE BLOSSOMS.

Deven smiles and says to me. Nihal has impeccable choice. I'm glad he chose you to come to see me.

I will share something with you. Nihal did suggest to me that you will be worthy, and I said that I will chose if you are worthy. On spending time with you I see that you are.

Come with me Andy. Let's go to a place in the research department.

It is something Nihal has as well but did not show you and said that you may not have been ready to experience this.

What you are about to see will make you want to learn and strive to perfect your science further. You will not need to though. Nihal and I have both agreed that when you are on our suns you are treated as an equal and we will share this with you.

Let us go.

A few minutes later we arrive at the research dept. The smell of burgers and tea fill the air. Still adjusting to that. Don't think I will ever though. I should suggest a milkshake in future.

Deven says "Andy we will make milkshakes in future. Tea is a bit ceremonious compared to the casual burger and milkshake. I will not be making any soda for you."

Deven the mind reader, interesting.

"Yes, deven that would be a perfect complement to the burgers. So, what is it that you want to show me?"

Andy, you have experienced teleportation. And on your own endeavours have contacted Nihal. Today you see time travel. I'm going to show you how vastly you have changed the entire solar system.

Your suggestion to get all the Sunlings back helped us get life to blossom for the first time.

I want to show you what this world would have looked like without that and what you have helped change it to.

Deven takes me into a room and all you see is screens on the walls.

He asks Kae to begin the time segment if I never arrived here.

All you see is the sun and planet after planet that is barren. The sun itself is red and eventually the Sunlings leave. A very horrible feeling for theses lovely happy beings.

Once this has run. Deven asks Kae to play the current projection of how life would turn out within this solar system and all you see on every planet is life. Trees, plants, animals on the land and abundant in clean oceans.

The planet is breath-taking. Looking to me like a computer creation more than anything.

"Deven how is this possible?"

"Andy, we have learnt to access the planets life projection. With no intervention all will be well here. Asteroids and other freak occurrences will occur, for now their future seems very stable and this is beautiful."

"How certain will this be?"

Given our proximity, almost 99% certain.

"Its like a fishbowl, the better it is cared for the greater chance your fish will be healthy"

So, if I wanted to go to this specific time would you be able to send me there?

"Excellent question Andy. I think it is highly possible, we can easily send a Sunlings. They have been studied for millennia. I would have to make some adjustments for a human. Consult with Nihal and I'm sure we can get you there.

Wow! A new sun and now I get to time travel. This is some adventure.

Andy let us return to my residence. I'm sure you need some rest. you have been up a while.

CHAPTER 10: TIME IS UP.

On reaching Devens home I shower and have a great rest. Waking many hours later to the voices of Dini and Simmi.

I can hear them discussing urgent news with Deven. I rub the sleep out of my eyes, get up, wash and head to see what's really going on.

Deven looks at me and you can see the sadness on his face.

He says that there is something horrible happening on Earth.

A pandemic has begun and Nihal has sent urgent news as he viewed the health of the planet. He asks if I could return to Earth immediately and make the necessary arrangements.

Suddenly, I hear my arm communicator beep and I see a message from Nihal...press the button when you are ready.

I gather my things .... Say goodbye and press the button.

Instantaneously transported to my home on earth and I switch on the news.

To find there has been an outbreak of a new disease in China.

THE END.